A CHINESE ZOO

HARCOURT BRACE JOVANOVICH, PUBLISHERS

SAN DIEGO   NEW YORK   LONDON

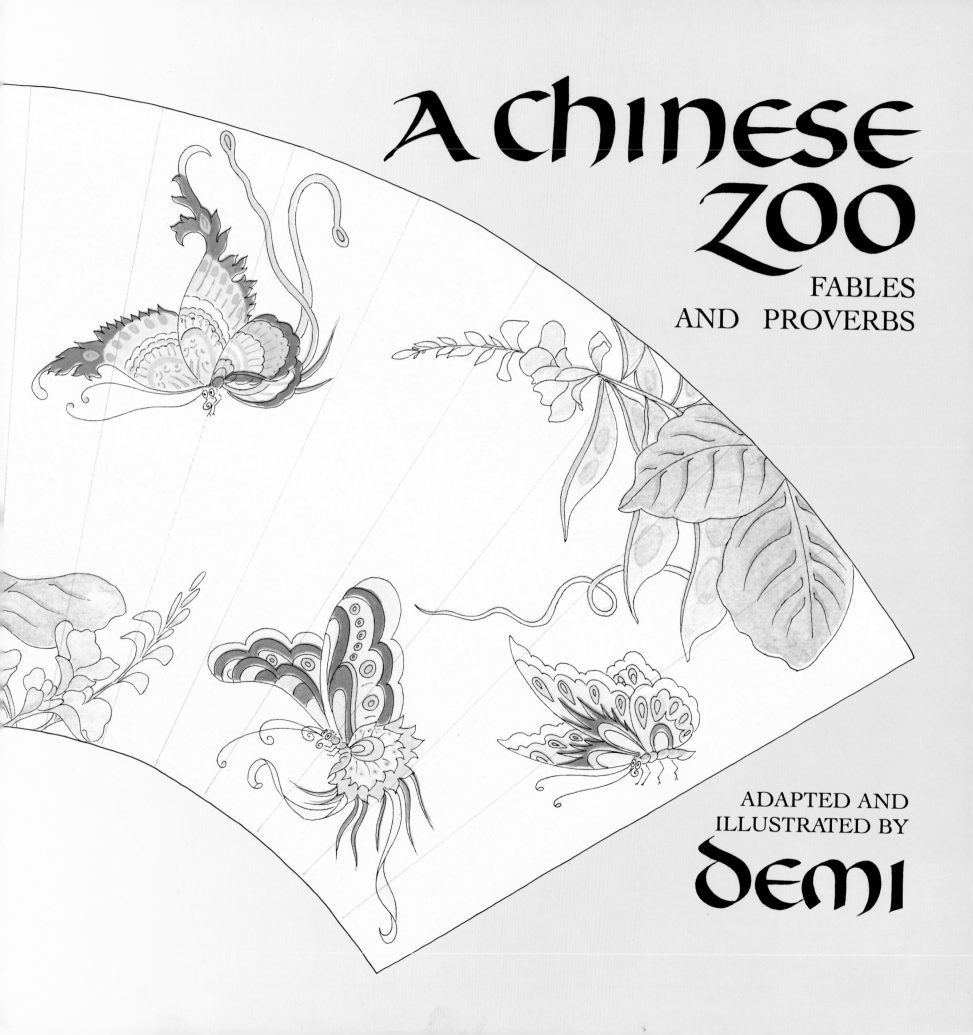

A Chinese ZOO

FABLES AND PROVERBS

ADAPTED AND
ILLUSTRATED BY

Demi

Requests for permission to make copies of any part of the work should be mailed to: Permissions, Harcourt Brace Jovanovich, Publishers, Orlando, Florida 32887.

The author and the publisher thank Random House for permission to retell three fables — the pandas in Heaven and Hell, the deer and the squirrel, and the artist's portrait of the Dragon Queen — from *Tales from Old China* by Isabelle C. Chang. In the Random House book these fables were titled "Heaven and Hell," "The World's Work," and "The Artist."

HBJ

Library of Congress Cataloging-in-Publication Data
Demi.
A Chinese zoo.
Summary: A collection of thirteen adapted Chinese fables, in which an array of animal characters demonstrate principles such as "It is foolish to be greedy" and "We frequently see only what we want to see."
1. Fables, Chinese. [1. Fables. 2. Folklore — China] I. Title.
PZ8.2.D3Ch 1987 398.2'0954 [E] 86-33562
ISBN 0-15-217510-5 Printed in Hong Kong First edition A B C D E

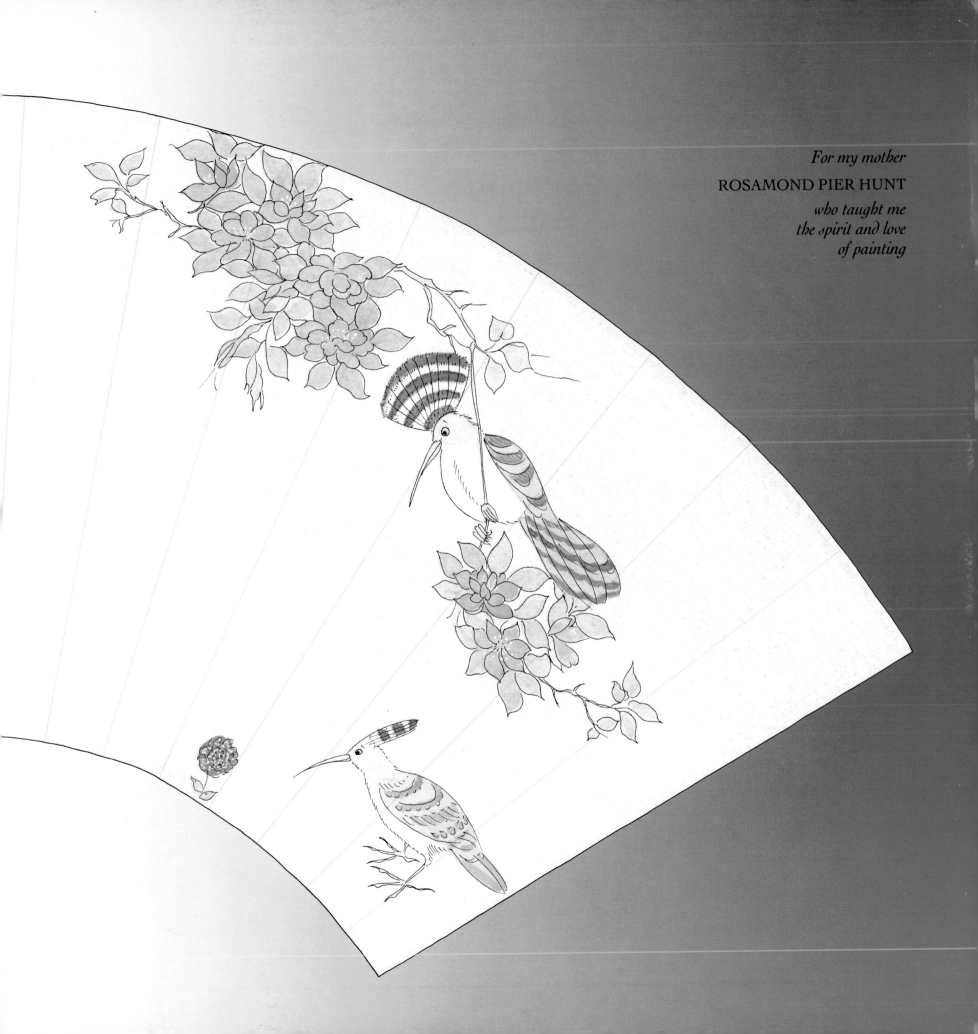

For my mother
ROSAMOND PIER HUNT
*who taught me
the spirit and love
of painting*

A hedgehog lost his favorite digging spade. He suspected the hedgehog who lived in a nearby hole. Not only did his neighbor look as though he had stolen the spade, but the noises he made sounded as though he had stolen the spade, and the way he hopped about seemed to prove without a doubt that he had stolen the spade.

A little while later, however, when the first hedgehog was digging up turnip roots with his paws, he happened to find the spade that he had lost.

Then, when he looked at the hedgehog who lived in the nearby hole, nothing about him looked as though he had stolen the spade.

Beware of judging by appearances.

Once upon a time there was a Monkey King who was very generous. He never rationed the chestnuts he gave to the animals throughout his kingdom, but then a blight hit all the trees and his supply dwindled. Afraid the monkeys might revolt if he reduced their food, the King issued a proclamation: "Each and every monkey will now receive three chestnuts in the morning and four in the evening."

朝三暮四

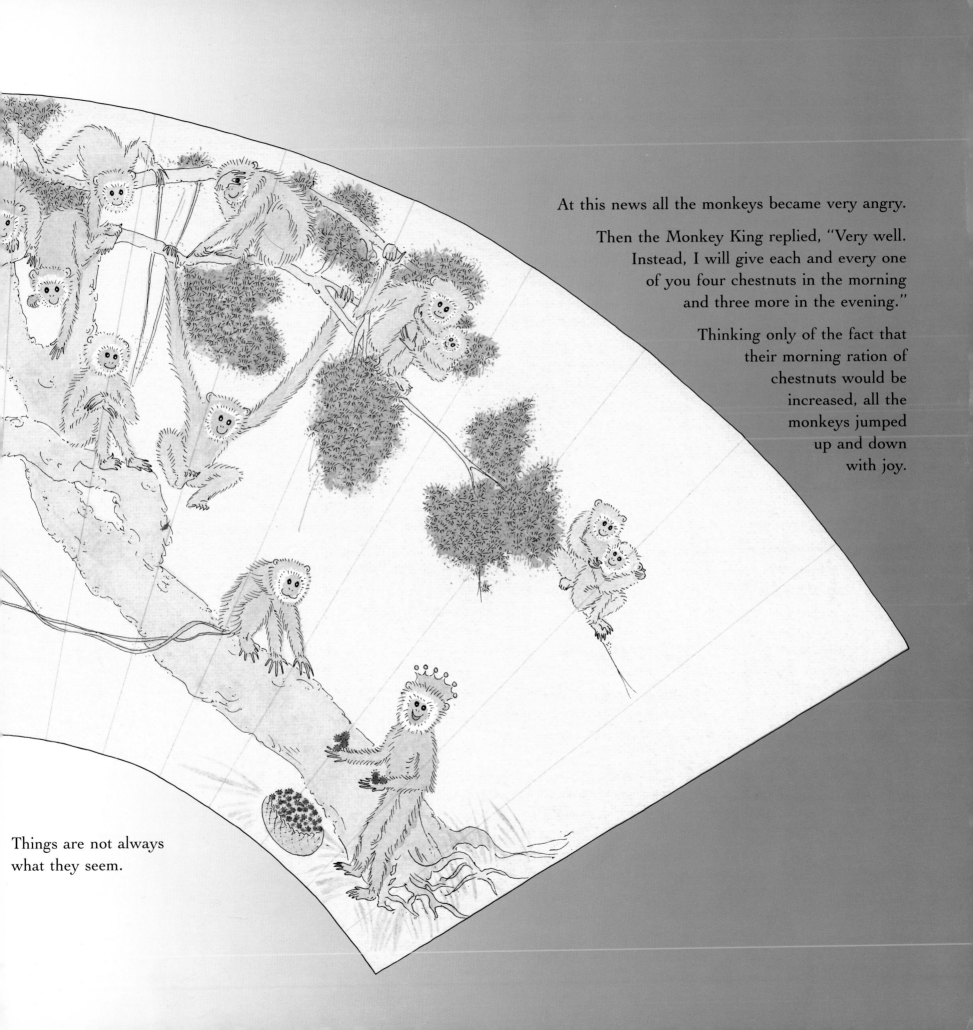

At this news all the monkeys became very angry.

Then the Monkey King replied, "Very well. Instead, I will give each and every one of you four chestnuts in the morning and three more in the evening."

Thinking only of the fact that their morning ration of chestnuts would be increased, all the monkeys jumped up and down with joy.

Things are not always what they seem.

A cat with prayer beads around his neck was sitting quietly and mewing softly. His eyes seemed tightly shut. Two mice saw him and were astonished that their enemy had suddenly become religious.

"That old cat has evidently changed his ways," they said. "He is saying his prayers. We don't have to worry about him anymore."

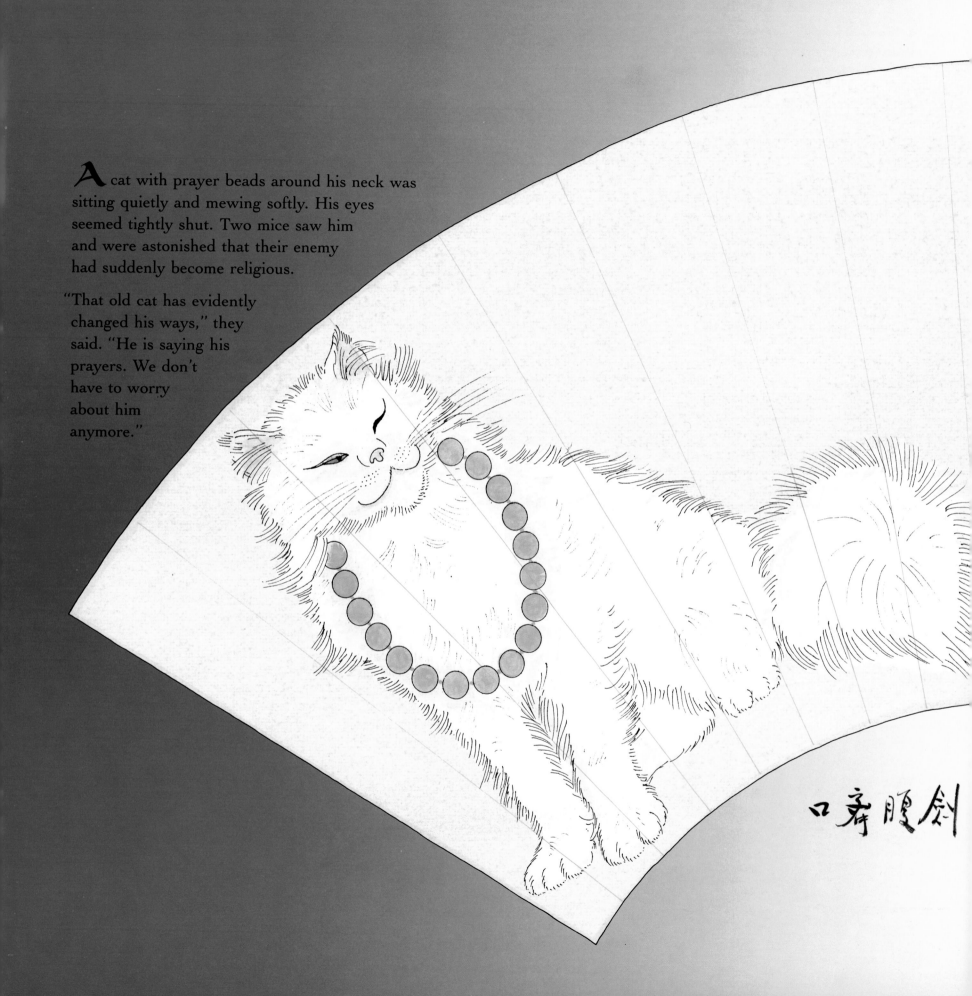

The two mice congratulated each other, jumped up and down, and began to play. They paid no attention to the cat, but when one mouse came too close, the sly cat immediately caught him and ate him. The other mouse, rushing home, said to himself, "Who would have believed that a cat who was busy saying his prayers would behave like that?"

Not all who make
a great show of devotion
can be trusted.

When the tiger was out hunting one day deep in the forest, he caught a fox.

As he prepared to eat his prey, the fox said to the tiger, "You must not eat me. I am the king of the forest. Come with me and I will show you how the other animals fear me."

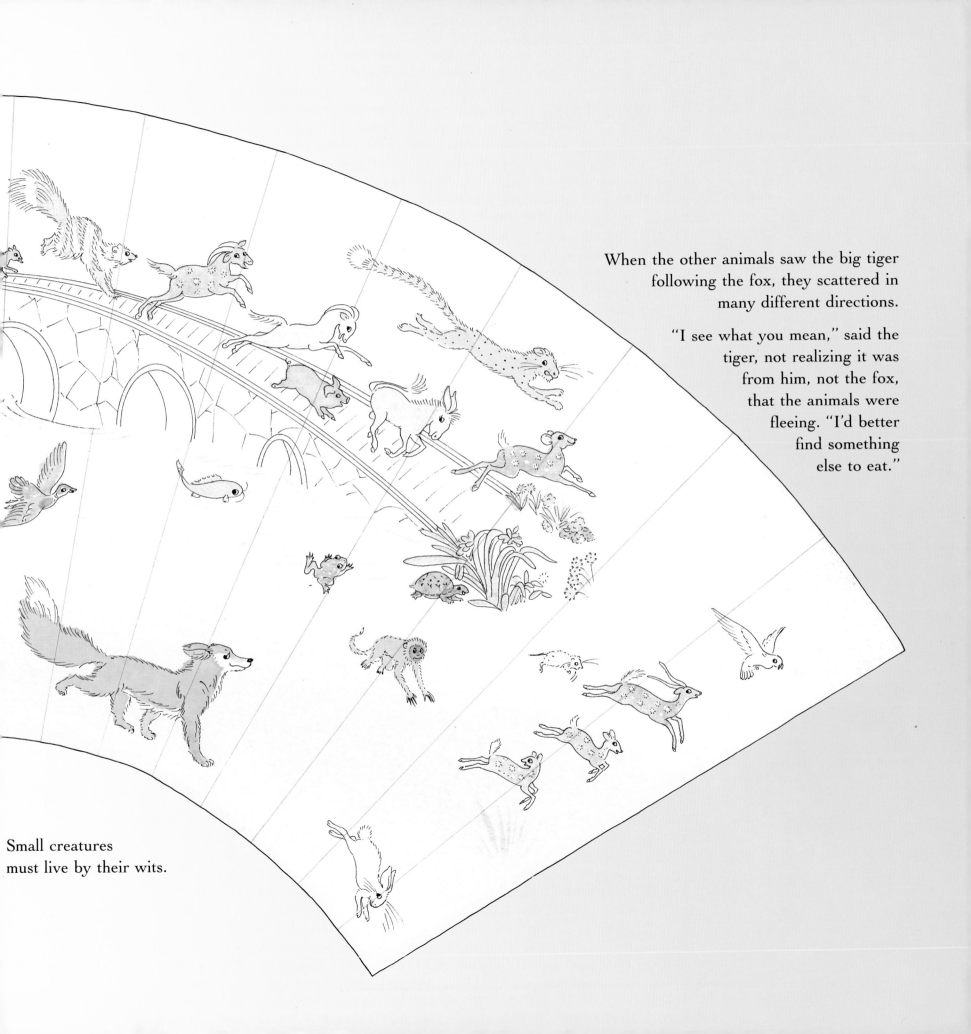

When the other animals saw the big tiger following the fox, they scattered in many different directions.

"I see what you mean," said the tiger, not realizing it was from him, not the fox, that the animals were fleeing. "I'd better find something else to eat."

Small creatures must live by their wits.

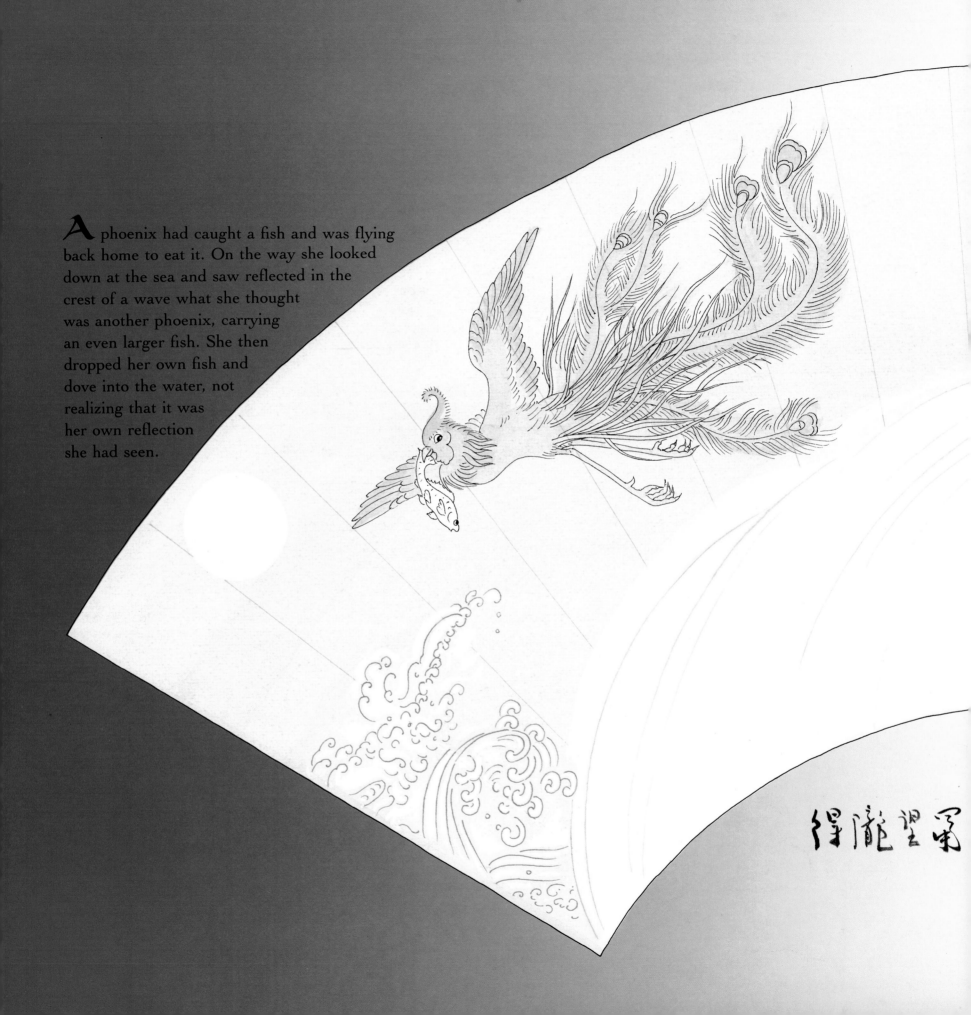

A phoenix had caught a fish and was flying back home to eat it. On the way she looked down at the sea and saw reflected in the crest of a wave what she thought was another phoenix, carrying an even larger fish. She then dropped her own fish and dove into the water, not realizing that it was her own reflection she had seen.

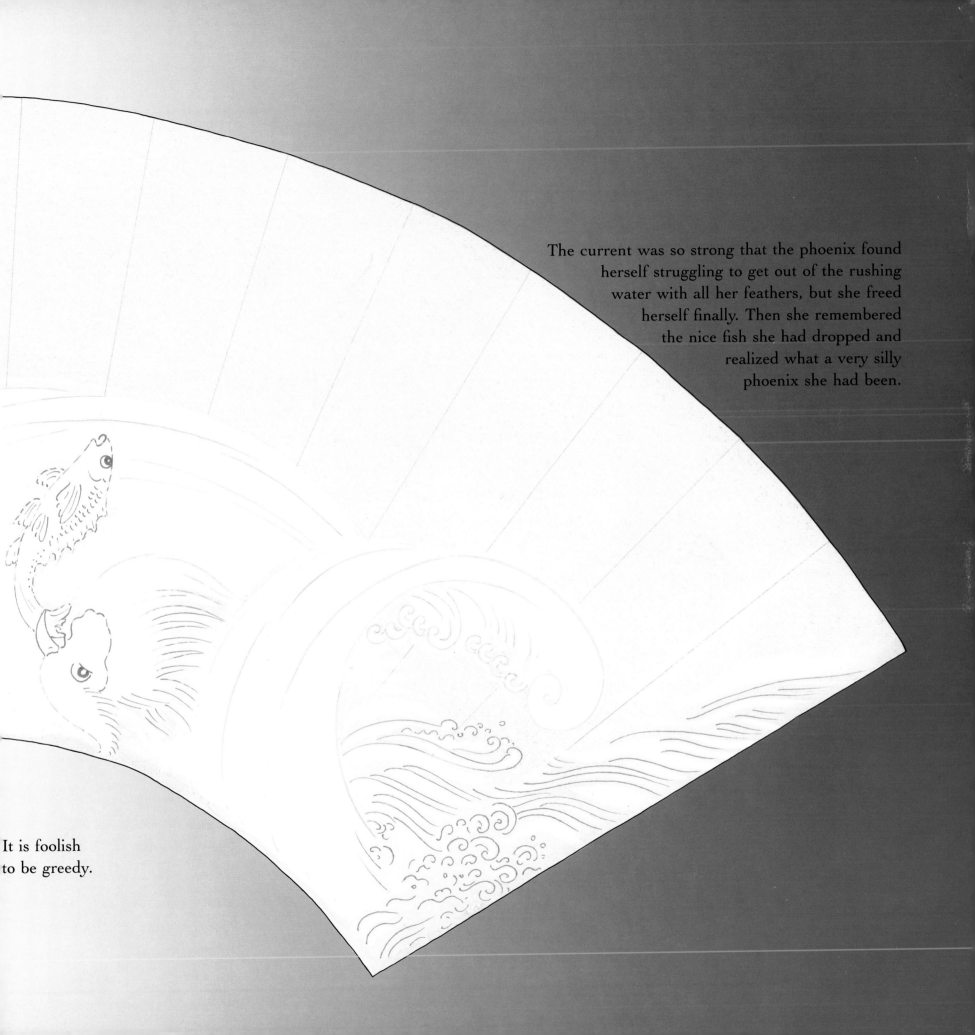

The current was so strong that the phoenix found
herself struggling to get out of the rushing
water with all her feathers, but she freed
herself finally. Then she remembered
the nice fish she had dropped and
realized what a very silly
phoenix she had been.

It is foolish
to be greedy.

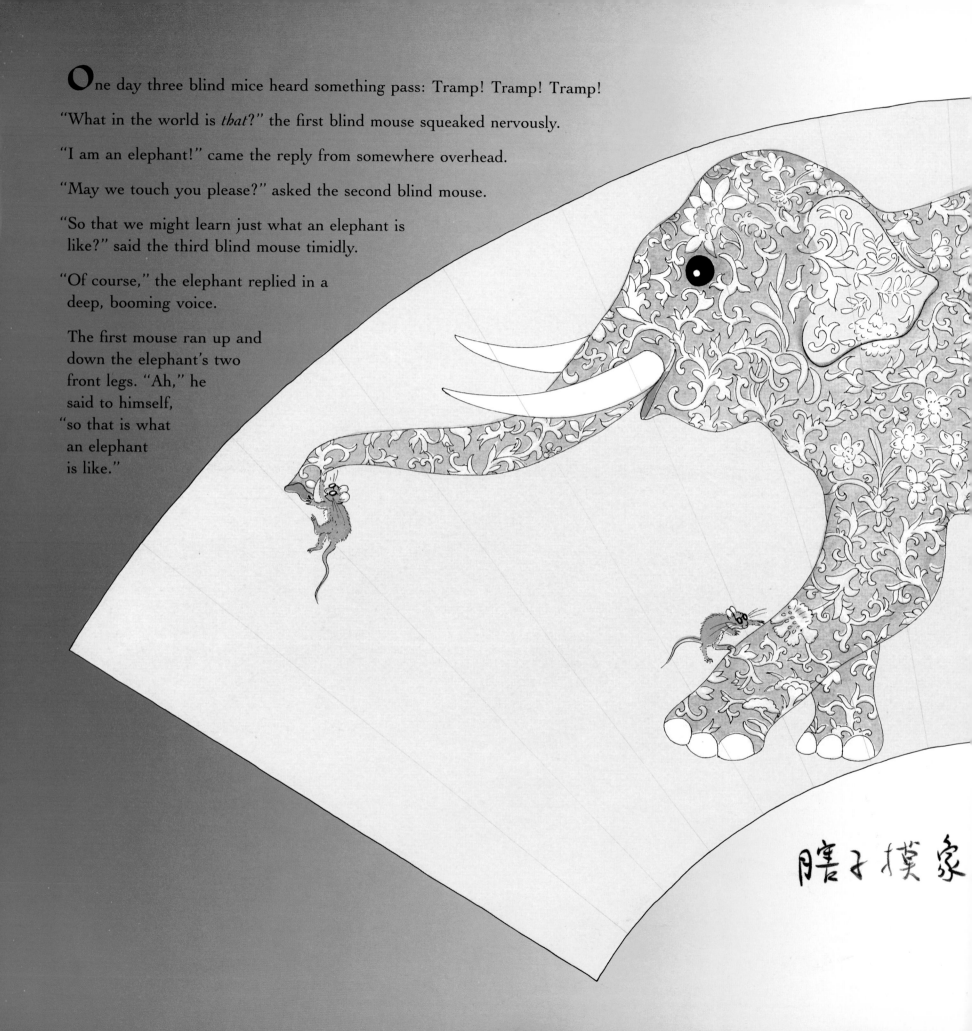

One day three blind mice heard something pass: Tramp! Tramp! Tramp!

"What in the world is *that*?" the first blind mouse squeaked nervously.

"I am an elephant!" came the reply from somewhere overhead.

"May we touch you please?" asked the second blind mouse.

"So that we might learn just what an elephant is like?" said the third blind mouse timidly.

"Of course," the elephant replied in a deep, booming voice.

The first mouse ran up and down the elephant's two front legs. "Ah," he said to himself, "so that is what an elephant is like."

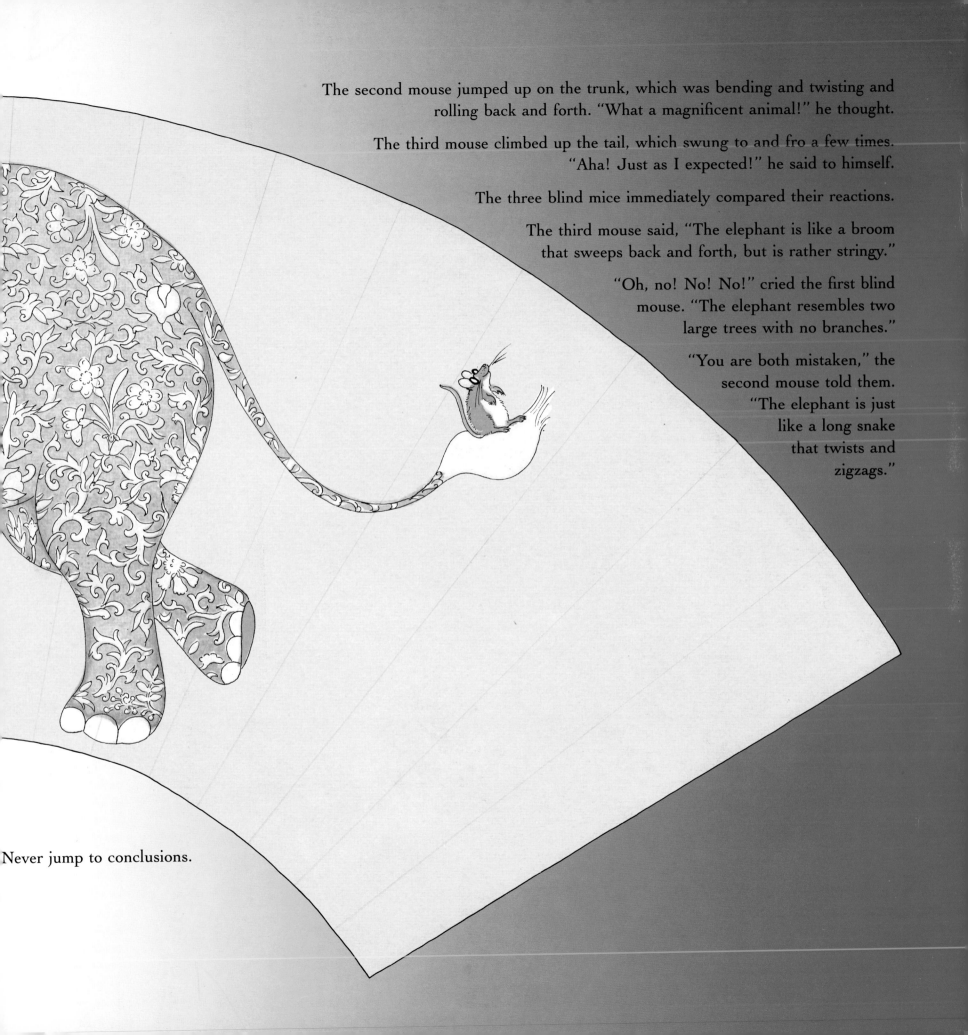

The second mouse jumped up on the trunk, which was bending and twisting and rolling back and forth. "What a magnificent animal!" he thought.

The third mouse climbed up the tail, which swung to and fro a few times. "Aha! Just as I expected!" he said to himself.

The three blind mice immediately compared their reactions.

The third mouse said, "The elephant is like a broom that sweeps back and forth, but is rather stringy."

"Oh, no! No! No!" cried the first blind mouse. "The elephant resembles two large trees with no branches."

"You are both mistaken," the second mouse told them. "The elephant is just like a long snake that twists and zigzags."

Never jump to conclusions.

One day a deer came upon a squirrel lying flat on his back with his feet in the air.

"Why are you doing that? What is wrong?" asked the deer.

"I was recently told that the great sky above is going to fall down," answered the squirrel.

"Foolish one!" replied the deer. "Perhaps a mighty dragon might be able to hold up the sky, but can you prop it up with just your two small feet?"

"Perhaps I can't hold all of it, but should I not try to hold up as much as I can?" answered the squirrel.

It is foolish to worry about everything you are told.

One day a big brown bear woke up and smelled some honey. Immediately he went outside and sniffed his way to a giant honeycomb, which was guarded by many bees. He bit off a huge chunk of the comb and ran off with it in his mouth. The bees buzzed right after him, and each one stung him on the nose.

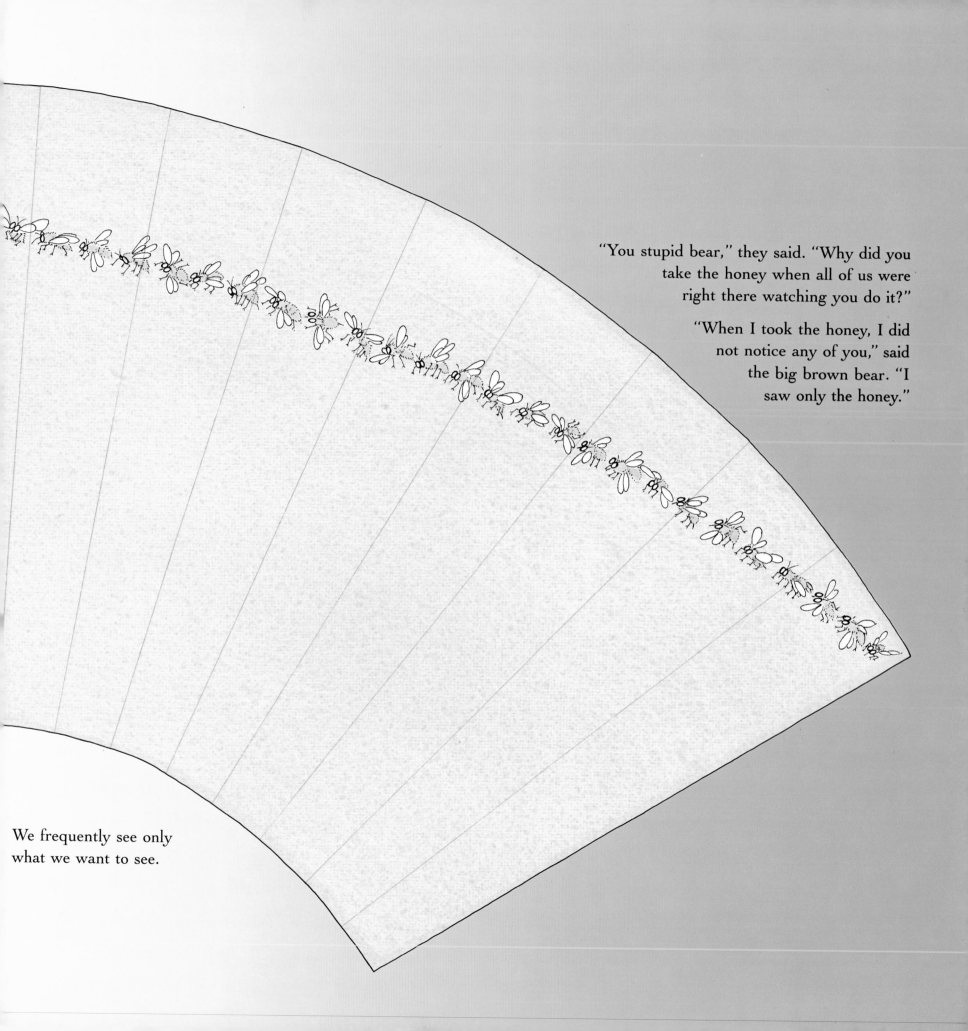

"You stupid bear," they said. "Why did you take the honey when all of us were right there watching you do it?"

"When I took the honey, I did not notice any of you," said the big brown bear. "I saw only the honey."

We frequently see only what we want to see.

A panda went to visit Hell. There he saw a large group of pandas growling and snarling. They were seated around a table with a hundred dishes of bamboo shoots, and beside each panda was a pair of chopsticks three feet long. But all the pandas were getting madder and madder and hungrier and hungrier because not one of them could figure out how to use the chopsticks to feed himself.

自食其果

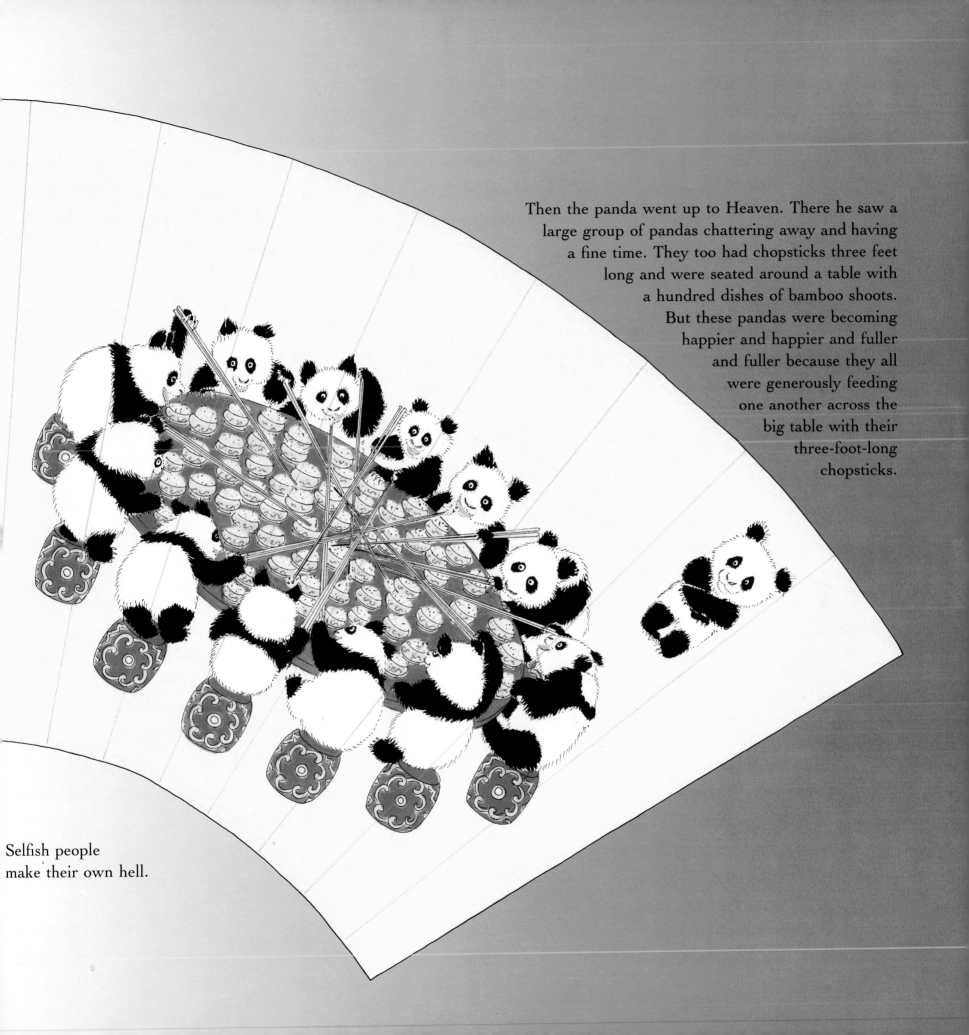

Then the panda went up to Heaven. There he saw a large group of pandas chattering away and having a fine time. They too had chopsticks three feet long and were seated around a table with a hundred dishes of bamboo shoots. But these pandas were becoming happier and happier and fuller and fuller because they all were generously feeding one another across the big table with their three-foot-long chopsticks.

Selfish people make their own hell.

There once was a mighty Dragon King who had a beautiful wife. "I really must have her picture painted," he thought to himself. Summoning his best court artist, he instructed him to paint a picture of the Dragon Queen.

The artist slithered up to his mountain studio, high above the clouds, took out his brushes and his silks, and began mixing his paints. He then embarked upon his task. Month after month went by, and the Dragon King heard nothing. Finally, flaming at the mouth, he charged up the mountain to the artist's studio and demanded to see the picture of his wife.

At once the artist unrolled some silk, took out his brushes, and quickly mixed his paints. In a flash a magnificent picture of the Queen emerged on the silk.

"If you can paint such a beautiful picture so quickly," roared the Dragon King, "why did you keep me waiting a whole year?"

Then the artist opened the back door of his studio. A whole mountain of discarded paintings were there: the Dragon Queen sitting, standing, running, rolling, roaring — the Queen pictured in every aspect of life.

"Your Majesty," explained the poor artist, "it took a year to learn how to paint a perfect picture of the Dragon Queen in a flash!"

No great thing is created suddenly.

One summer day a clam came out of the water to sun himself on the sand. A young crane, spotting him from above, thought what a tasty meal he would make. Flying down, the crane tried to take the clam out of his shell, but the clam clamped down, trapping the crane's beak inside.

The young crane tugged and tugged but could not free his beak, while the clam, of course, was unable to get back into the water.

Time passed, but neither would give in.

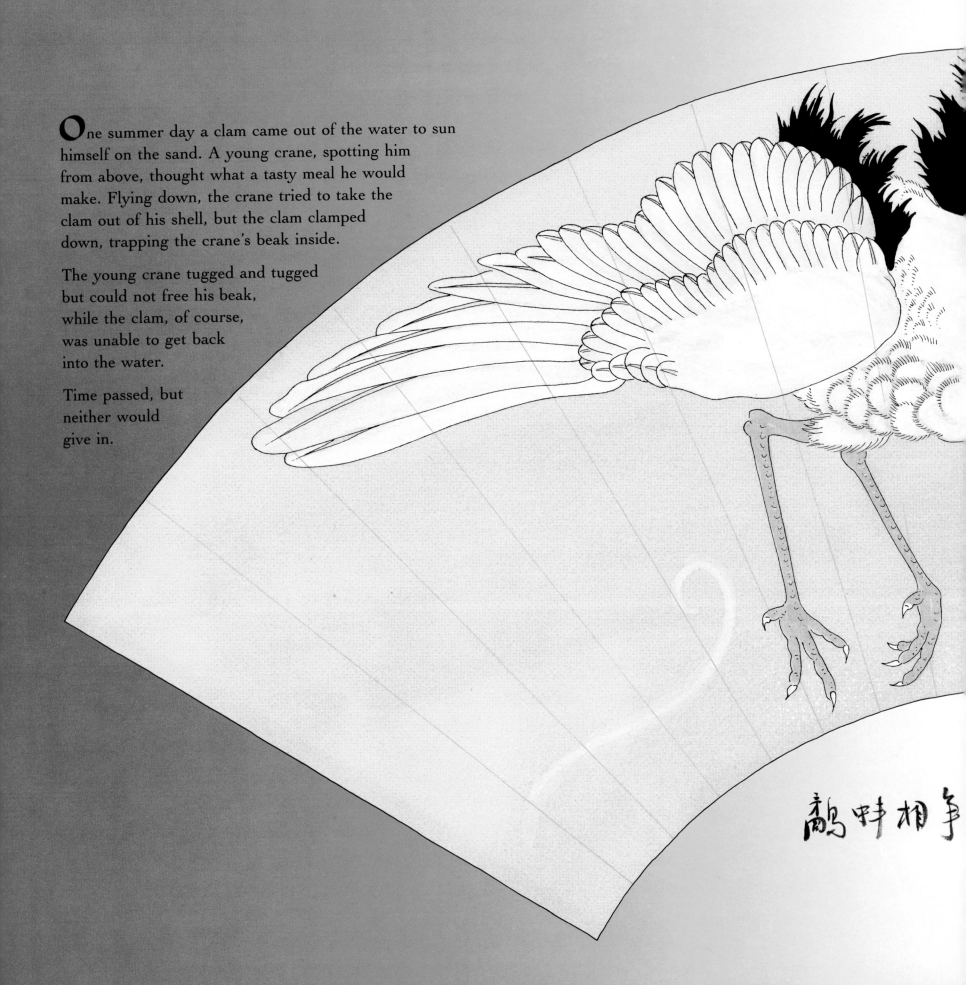

鷸蚌相争

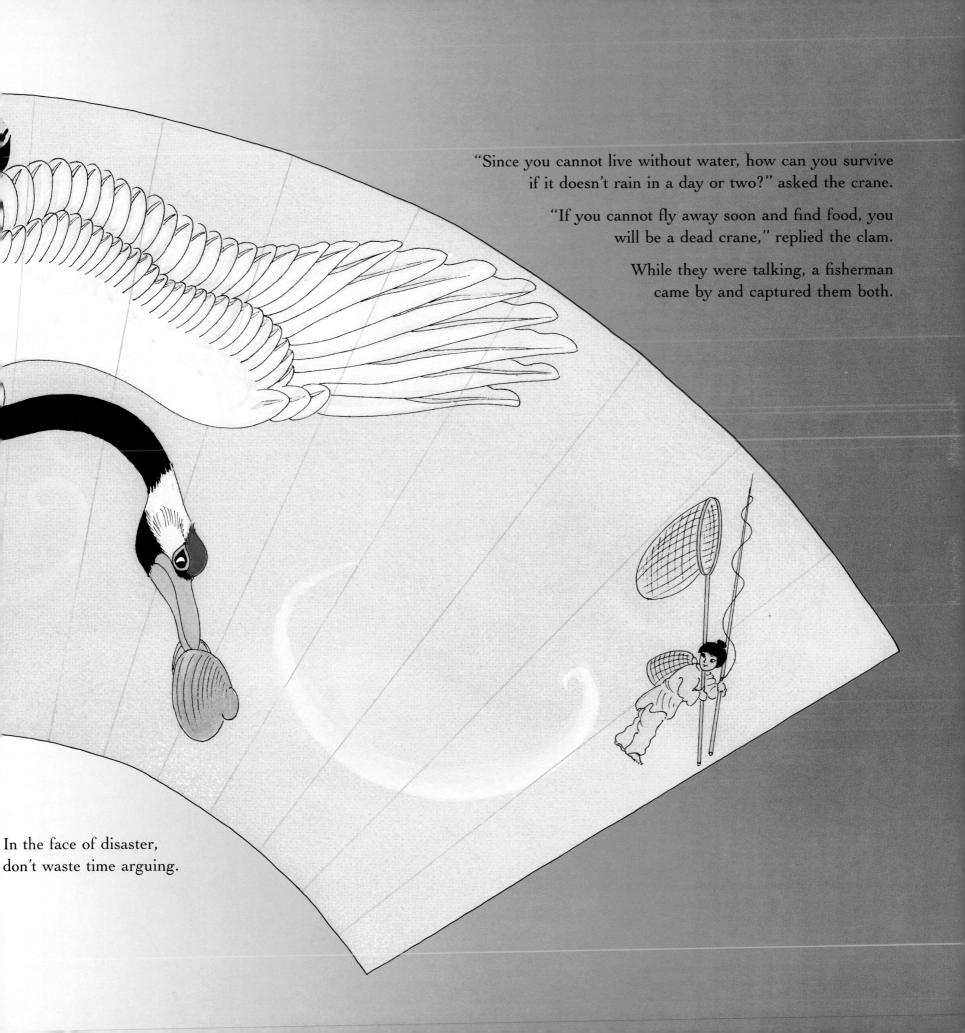

"Since you cannot live without water, how can you survive
if it doesn't rain in a day or two?" asked the crane.

"If you cannot fly away soon and find food, you
will be a dead crane," replied the clam.

While they were talking, a fisherman
came by and captured them both.

In the face of disaster,
don't waste time arguing.

One day a wolf was hunting in the forest. He was growing weary, having been at the job for a very long time without catching anything to eat.

Suddenly a rabbit ran into a tree and fell over dead. Picking up the rabbit, the wolf carried it home and had a delicious meal.

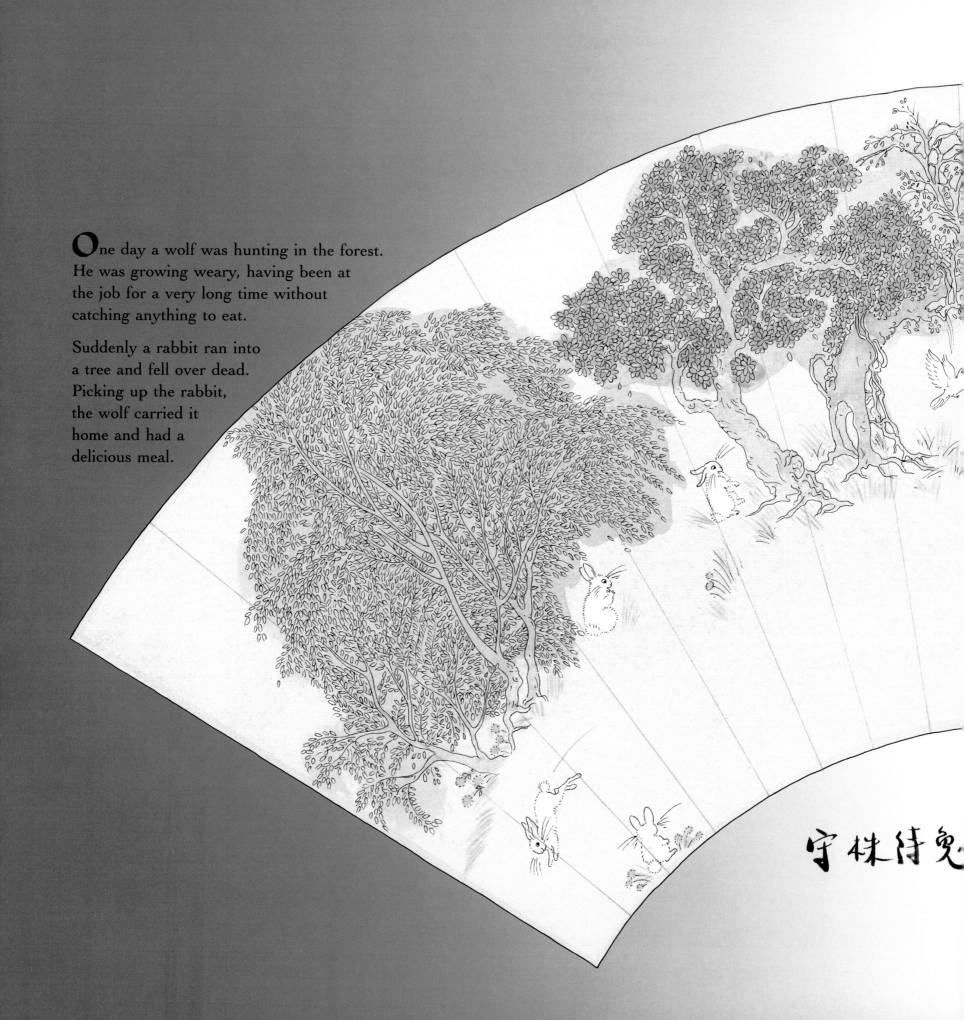

"Why should I walk miles a day through the forest looking for food when I could sit by that tree and catch a rabbit every day?" he said to himself.

The next day, he took up his post by the tree, but though he sat there for days and days, no other rabbit ever ran into it.

It is not wise to trust to chance.

While two unicorns were playing together along a path deep in the forest, they came upon a mighty lion. The bigger unicorn, ignoring his small friend, leaped up to the highest branch of a tree. The little unicorn, who could not jump very high, fell to the ground and pretended to be dead.

The lion then bent over the small figure, seemed to whisper something in the little unicorn's ear, and went on his way.

From up in the highest branch of the tree, the bigger
unicorn asked, "What did the lion say to you?"

"He told me," the little unicorn replied, "that
he was not hungry, for he'd just eaten,
and that in the future I should not
count on friends who care only
for themselves."

A true friend
is a treasure.

These fables are based on ancient Chinese sources, though most fables can be traced back originally to the Indian *Jataka Tales* or *The Panchatantra*. When the fables were introduced into China, however, they inevitably were changed, and some of the Chinese fables we know today date back as far as the seventh century B.C., while others are believed to be as recent as the seventeenth century. They are an interwoven part of the thinking, the history, and the daily lives of the people.

The Chinese calligraphy was painted by Tze-si "Jesse" Huang in the Ts'ao-Shu, or Flying Grass, Style. Executed with incredible speed and freedom, every character has an inherent and visible link with the rest, and the spirit and character of the artist is in every stroke.

The fans were painted on English watercolor papers with Chinese brushes consisting of the autumn hairs of rabbit, sheep, goat, and tiger, with handles of tortoise, blackwood, and rhinoceros horn.

The text type was set in Cochin on Linotron 202 by Thom Type, San Diego, California.
The display type was hand-lettered by Jeanyee Wong.
Printed and bound by South China Printing Company, Quarry Bay, Hong Kong
Production supervision by Warren Wallerstein and Rebecca Miller
Designed by Barbara DuPree Knowles